A Giant First-Start Reader

This easy reader contains only 54 different words, repeated often to help the young reader develop word recognition and interest in reading.

Basic word list for *Here Comes Jack Frost*

a	goes	swirl
again	has	swirls
and	he	tap
away	here	the
blows	him	them
brushes	his	then
but	Jack	they
cold	look	to
come	makes	tonight
comes	night	until
curl	on	up
curls	out	very
down	paints	when
every	person	will
for	road	wind
from	see	window
Frost	special	you
go	sun	your

Here Comes Jack Frost

Written by Sharon Peters

Illustrated by Eulala Connor

Troll Associates

Library of Congress Cataloging in Publication Data

Peters, Sharon.
   Here comes Jack Frost.

   Summary: When the wind blows on a cold night, Jack
Frost goes-to work.
   [1. Jack Frost—Fiction]   I. Connor, Eulala.
II. Title.
PZ7.P44183He   [E]   81-4093
ISBN 0-89375-513-3   AACR2
ISBN 0-89375-514-1 (pbk.)

Look out your window.
On a cold night you will see him.

When the cold wind blows you will see him.

Look out your window.

Look for a very special person.

You will see Jack Frost!

He goes down the road.

He goes to your window.

Out come his paints.

Out come his brushes.

Tap, tap, tap, on your window.

He makes a curl.

He makes a swirl.

Jack Frost paints swirls and curls on your window.

He goes from window to window.

Until every window has swirls and curls.

Then away go his paints.

Away go his brushes.

Jack Frost goes down the road.

Jack Frost goes away.

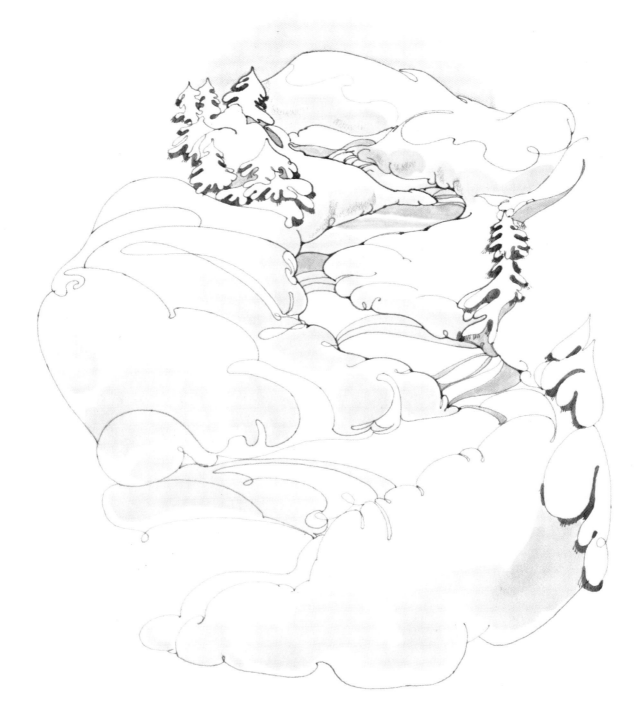

When the sun comes up, you will see them.

You will see swirls and curls on your window.

But then they go away.

The swirls and curls go away.

But tonight, when the cold wind
blows, you will see him.

Look out your window.

Look for a very special person.

You will see Jack Frost again!

Tap, tap, tap.